The Invisible Dog

Dick King-Smith served in the Grenadier Guards during the Second World War, and afterwards spent twenty years as a farmer in Gloucestershire, the county of his birth. Many of his stories are inspired by his farming experiences. Later he taught at a village primary school. His first book, *The Fox Busters*, was published in 1978. Since then he has written a great number of children's books, including *The Sheep-Pig* (winner of the *Guardian* Award and filmed as *Babe*), *Harry's Mad, Noah's Brother, The Hodgeheg, Martin's Mice, Ace, The Cuckoo Child* and *Harriet's Hare* (winner of the Children's Book Award in 1995). At the British Book Awards in 1992 he was voted Children's Author of the Year. He is married, with three children and eleven grandchildren, and lives in a seventeenth-century cottage a short crow's-flight from the house where he was born.

DICK KING-SMITH

THE
INVISIBLE DOG

Illustrated by Paul Howard

PUFFIN BOOKS

PUFFIN BOOKS

Published by the Penguin Group
Penguin Books Ltd, 80 Strand, London WC2R 0RL, England
Penguin Putnam Inc., 375 Hudson Street, New York, New York 10014, USA
Penguin Books Australia Ltd, Ringwood, Victoria, Australia
Penguin Books Canada Ltd, 10 Alcorn Avenue, Toronto, Ontario, Canada M4V 3B2
Penguin Books India (P) Ltd, 11 Community Centre, Panchsheel Park, New Delhi – 110 017, India
Penguin Books (NZ) Ltd, Cnr Rosedale and Airborne Roads, Albany, Auckland, New Zealand
Penguin Books (South Africa) (Pty) Ltd, 24 Sturdee Avenue, Rosebank 2196 South Africa

Penguin Books Ltd, Registered Offices: 80 Strand, London WC2R 0RL, England

www.penguin.com

First published by Viking 1995
Published in Puffin Books 1997
23

Text copyright © Fox Busters Ltd, 1995
Illustrations copyright © Paul Howard, 1995
All rights reserved

The moral right of the author has been asserted

Filmset in Palatino

Made and printed in England by Clays Ltd, St Ives plc

British Library Cataloguing in Publication Data
A CIP catalogue record for this book is available from the British Library

ISBN 0–140–34994–4

Contents

1. The Lead and Collar

Rupert died when Janie was only two, so that she didn't really remember anything about him.

She knew what he looked like, of course – there were lots of photos of him:

on his own, or with Mum or Dad, and one she specially liked of herself as a toddler sitting on the lawn with Rupert standing beside her. She was just sorry she'd never known him.

"Mum," Janie said one day, "how long ago did Rupert die?"

"Oh, let's see," her mother said. "He died when you were two and now you're seven. So – five years ago."

"And how old was he?"

"He was eight."

"That's not very old for a dog, is it?" Janie said.

"Not for most dogs," her mother said, "but then Rupert was very big, a giant really. Great Danes don't usually live as long as smaller dogs."

"What did he die of?"

"Kidney failure."

"Were you and Daddy sad?"

"Terribly."

"Is that why we've never had a dog since?"

"I suppose it is, really. We talked about getting a puppy, but somehow it seemed as though no other dog could replace Rupert, so we never did."

"What kind of puppy would you have got?" asked Janie.

"Oh, a Great Dane again, I think. We wouldn't want any other sort of dog. But they're awfully expensive to buy and awfully expensive to keep."

"Shall we ever have another one, d'you think?"

"I don't know, darling," Janie's mother said. "We'll see."

"We'll see", Janie knew, always meant "probably not and don't go pestering me about it or it'll be certainly not". So she thought she'd better drop the subject.

However, the spirit of the late great Rupert must have decided otherwise, for only a few days later Janie came by chance upon something she'd never set eyes on before.

She was hunting about at the back of the garage, where her father had his workbench, looking for an oil-can to oil her bike, when she saw something hanging high on a nail in a dark dusty corner.

It was a dog-collar with a lead attached.

Janie climbed up on to the bench and took it down.

The collar was a very big, broad, brass-studded one with a round metal disc attached to the buckle. She rubbed the disc clear of dust and there, scratched on the face, was the name RUPERT and, underneath, their telephone number.

Janie put the collar to her nose. It smelt

of leather and dog, and just for a
moment it made her feel sad to think that
this faint smell was all that was left of the
creature whose great neck the collar had
encircled. How many hundreds of times
in his eight years of life would he have
gone for a walk wearing it, with Mum or
Dad holding the end of the thick plaited
lead.

Janie went out of the garden gate and wandered up the lane, the loop of the lead in her left hand, the empty collar dangling. She looked down at the thick leather circlet and imagined the shape and sweep of the great neck, the Great Dane neck, within it. She saw the dog clearly in her mind's eye as it walked beside her.

Lost in a daydream, she almost bumped into Mrs Garrow, an elderly widow who lived alone in one of the cottages at the top end of the village.

"Hullo, Janie! Where are you off to then?" said the old lady with a loud laugh. Mrs Garrow's laugh sounded like nothing so much as a duck quacking.

"I'm taking my dog for a walk," Janie said.

"I can see that," said Mrs Garrow, and she put out a hand and patted the air behind the dangling collar, just where the dog's back would have been.

"Who's a good boy then?" said Mrs Garrow. "He's looking ever so well, Janie; you must be proud of him. Make sure you keep him on the lead, mind; there's a lot of traffic in the lane these days," and she went on her way, quacking loudly.

Some people never grow too old for games of make-believe, thought Janie. That's nice. And two can play at that.

"Heel!" she said, and she walked on, the invisible dog pacing at her side.

2. The Name

After Janie had gone to bed that night, her parents were talking.

"I see Janie's got hold of old Rupert's collar and lead," her father said.

"Yes," her mother said. "She's been carrying it around all day. It's lying beside her bed now."

"When I arrived home from work," her father said, "she was so engrossed with it I don't think she even heard the car. She was walking round the lawn, dangling the collar and talking away to an imaginary animal. Every now and then she'd stop and say 'Sit!' and then after a bit she'd say 'Heel!' and walk on again."

"I know. I can only think she must have a very vivid imagination to play a game like that for so long."

"Has she been pestering you to get a puppy?"

"No. It would be nice though, David, wouldn't it? One day."

"Another Great Dane?"

"Of course."

"Oh, come off it, Sally," Janie's father said. "They're awfully expensive to buy and awfully expensive to keep. I mean, these days a decent Dane puppy costs over three hundred pounds."

"You know that, do you?"

"Well . . . yes, I just happened to notice an advertisement. And as for feeding a growing pup – well, you can reckon on over six hundred pounds a year."

"So we can't afford one?"

"No. You weren't seriously thinking of getting one?"

"No."

"Right then."

At breakfast next morning they both noticed that the loop of the lead was round Janie's left wrist as she ate, the collar on the floor beside her.

"Do we have to have that dirty old thing at table?" her father asked.

"He's not a dirty old thing," Janie said.

"He? I'm talking about the collar and lead."

"Oh sorry, Dad, I thought you were talking about my dog."

"It's a funny thing," her mother said, "but Daddy and I can't actually *see* a dog."

"You wouldn't," said Janie. "He's invisible."

"I see."

"No you don't, Mum."

"I mean, I hear what you're saying. By the way, what do you feed him on?"

"Invisible food."

"In an invisible dish?"

"Naturally."

"Think of the money you're saving," Janie's father said, "never having to fork out for dog-meat or biscuits. Can't cost you a penny."

"Of course it does, Daddy. When we

go shopping today, you wouldn't believe
how much I shall have to spend."

"Invisible money?"

"Of course."

"Has he got a name, this invisible
dog?" her mother asked.

"Well, no, not yet," said Janie. "I haven't decided."

"Have you decided what breed he is?" her father said.

"Oh honestly, Daddy!" said Janie. "I should have thought that you'd have known a Great Dane when you saw one."

"You could just call him Rupert," her

mother said. "That's what's written on his collar, after all."

"No," said Janie. "I think this dog ought to have a different name, don't you?"

"Oh yes," they said.

"I mean, he's quite a different colour, isn't he?"

"Is he?" they said.

"Rupert was a fawn dog, with a black mask," Janie's father said.

"Whereas this one," Janie's mother said, "is . . . um . . . well . . . what would you say, Janie?"

"Black with white splodges," said Janie. "Or white with black splodges, whichever you like to say."

"A harlequin Great Dane!" they cried. "Of course."

"So he really needs a sort of black-and-white name, doesn't he?"

"Like Magpie, you mean?" said her mother.

"Or Zebra," said her father.

"Or Panda."

"Or Penguin."

"Yes," said Janie, "but I don't like any of those names. I think I'll just call him Spotty."

"You can't!" they cried with one voice. "You can't call a harlequin Great Dane 'Spotty'. It's not dignified enough."

"He's my dog," said Janie, and she put down a hand and stroked an invisible back, "so I can call you Spotty if I want to, or Tom, Dick or Harry."

"He liked 'Harry'," said Janie's father, looking down at the collar lying on the floor. "He wagged his tail a bit when you said 'Harry'."

Janie's mother raised her eyes to heaven.

"Oh honestly, David!" she said.
"You're as bad as she is. No doubting
where she gets it from."

"Harry," said Janie. "I quite like that."

"Or perhaps Henry," said her father.
"That's a bit more dignified."

"Henry?" said Janie. "Henry! Yes,
you're right, Daddy. He's wagging his
tail like mad now. Henry it is!"

3. The Price

All this happened towards the end of the holidays, and as the new term approached, Janie's parents began to wonder if Henry would be taken to school.

They worried at the thought of their child doing lessons or playing games or eating her lunch, always attached to the lead and collar. It was all very well to make-believe at home, but whatever would the teachers think?

They waited, a little nervously, for the first day of term.

"Got all your school things ready?" her father said at breakfast.

"Yes."

Her mother drew a deep breath.

"You're not taking Henry, are you, darling?" she said.

"Oh honestly, Mummy!" said Janie. "You know we're not allowed pets at school, not even a gerbil, let alone a Great Dane. But he can come in the car with us, can't he?"

"Oh. Yes. Of course."

"And then he can go back home with

you once you've dropped Daddy off at the station."

"All right."

"You'll have to exercise him, Mum."

"Take him for a walk, d'you mean?" her mother asked nervously.

"No, just let him out for a run in the garden. Mind you take his lead off or he'll trip over it. Just let him out at lunch time, that'll be enough. After all, we don't want Henry making a mess in the house. Specially an invisible mess."

"I wonder what it would be like," said her father thoughtfully, "stepping in an invisible dog-mess?"

When, however, her mother drove to fetch Janie at the end of the school day, she found that she had forgotten something. As they came out of the playground and reached the car, parked

30

at the roadside, Janie looked in at the back seat and made a little noise of disappointment.

"Oh, Mum!" she said. "You left Henry at home."

Janie's mother stopped herself on the verge of saying, "No, he's there all right, it's just that he's invisible." From then on she was always careful, whenever she collected Janie, to have put the collar at one or other end of the back seat and the lead ready for Janie to clip on when they arrived home.

"Have you told them at school?" Janie's mum said, a few days later.

"Told who?"

"Your friends."

"What about?"

"About Henry."

"No. But I told our teacher," said Janie.

"What! That we'd got a Great Dane?"

"No. Just that we might have one, one day. Another one, I mean, as well as Henry."

"What makes you think that?"

"Well, we might, Mum, mightn't we? You never know what's going to happen."

"I do," her mother said, "and we aren't. Your father wouldn't consider it."

"How d'you know?"

"You ask him."

So when her father came home from work that evening, Janie did.

She didn't for one moment think that he'd say yes, though she half hoped for a "We'll see", which would mean there might be a chance, but he simply said, "No, of course not. Can't afford it."

"How much would a puppy cost

then?" Janie said. "A Great Dane puppy, I mean. A harlequin Great Dane."

Her father stopped himself on the verge of saying "three hundred pounds". Possibly that was a guess on the low side, he thought, and probably harlequins are more expensive than other colours, and anyway, if I say a really high price she'll forget the whole silly business.

"Five hundred pounds," he said.

Janie looked down at the collar, dangling as usual from its lead, and patted an invisible head.

"D'you hear that, Henry?" she said. "Just think what you must be worth."

"You stick to Henry," her father said.

"I could save up my pocket money," Janie said.

"Take you about ten years."

"Just think! I'd be seventeen," said

Janie, "nearly eighteen, and then I'd be grown up and you wouldn't be able to stop me buying a Great Dane puppy."

"I'm not stopping *you* buying one now," her father said. "Just so long as you've got the money. You come along with five hundred pounds and then . . . "

"And then what, Daddy?"

"Then we'll see."

4. The Show

Janie's birthday was in the early part of January, and for a treat each year she was always taken to London – to the Zoo, or Madame Tussaud's, or the Tower, or the Natural History Museum.

"What shall we do for Janie's birthday outing this year?" her mother said. "Can you think of something a bit out of the ordinary?"

"As a matter of fact, I can," Janie's father said.

"What?"

"Cruft's."

"Cruft's Dog Show?"

"Yes. Might be rather fun, don't you think?"

"Which day? It's a four-day show, I seem to remember.

"Oh, the fourth day, I think."

"Why? No, don't tell me, David; I can read you like a book. Great Danes are judged on the fourth day. That's it, isn't it?"

"Well, yes. I mean, I know they're your favourite breed, Sally."

"Not by any chance yours too?"

38

"Well, yes. But I just thought it might be fun for Janie."

"I see. Don't you think it might be a bit hard on the child? She may not be satisfied with an invisible Great Dane. It isn't as if you had any intention of buying a puppy."

"No," said her husband. "Though I told Janie *she* could buy one."

"You did *what*?"

"I said that if she came along with five hundred pounds clutched in her hot little hand, then I wouldn't stop her buying a Dane puppy."

"You say the stupidest things sometimes. Next thing you know, she'll be robbing a bank."

"Well, shall we go to Cruft's or shan't we?"

"Ask Janie."

"A dog show?" Janie said when the

idea was put to her. "What dog show?"

"Cruft's. The biggest of them all. There'll probably be something like 20,000 dogs there altogether. Of every breed."

"Great Danes?"

"Of course."

"Harlequin Great Danes like Henry?"

"Sure to be some. Though they'll look a bit different from Henry."

"Why?"

"Well, you can't see him too well."

"Can he come to Cruft's?"

"No."

"Poor old boy," said Janie, fondling an invisible ear. "I'll tell you all about it afterwards."

Apart from those old snapshots of Rupert, Janie had never in her life set eyes upon a Great Dane until that unforgettable day shortly after her eighth birthday. They had walked into the great hall of Olympia and made their way past the judging of a whole lot of other breeds – terriers and collies and gun dogs and many more – and suddenly there were the giants, a ring full of them.

Black and blue, fawn and brindle and harlequin, they stood and showed themselves in all their majestic dignity.

The judge was a little woman, small enough, it seemed to Janie, to have gone for a ride on any one of the great dogs whose points she was so carefully examining.

Janie and her mother and father watched at the ringside as class succeeded class, and handlers stood their charges before the little judge, or walked or ran around the ring, the huge dogs striding out beside them. Tall men or

short men, thin ladies or fat, old or young, they each had something in common, thought Janie – a Great Big Beautiful Dane. If only we could have one some day, she said to herself.

A man beside them noticed the rapt expression on Janie's face.

"Bet you wish you had a dog like one of those," he said with a smile.

"Actually," said Janie, "I have. He's called Henry."

"Imagine that!" said the friendly man.

"Henry's rather out of the ordinary," Janie's mother said.

"Out of this world," said her father.

They stayed and watched till the end of the judging, till the little woman had made her choice between Best Dog and Best Bitch. Both appeared equally beautiful to Janie – every one of the Danes there, it seemed to her, were faultless; she couldn't see any difference between them except colour. But she

desperately wanted the dog to win Best of Breed because, just by chance, he was a harlequin. And her wish was granted.

"He's beautiful!" Janie said.

"Isn't he just!"

"They all were."

"Weren't they just!"

Afterwards they went round the benches, and there he was, with his rosettes and his prize cards and his proud owner.

Janie pushed between a small crowd of admirers to get a closer look. The dog, she could see, knew just what a clever fellow he was. He had a kind of smile on his great face and his long tail wagged slowly and majestically.

"He's called Champion Larkmeadow Nobleman of Merlincourt," she told her parents.

"Gosh! What a mouthful."

"But his owner called him Bob. I heard him."

"That's better."

"Funny thing though," said Janie.

"What?"

"He looked just *exactly* like Henry."

5. The Tea-leaves

The postbox was at the top end of the village, not much more than a hundred yards from Janie's front gate. It was, in fact, set into the low garden wall of Mrs Garrow's cottage, and Janie sometimes wondered how the old lady posted any letters she might write. Did she come out into the lane and post them from the front like everyone else, or did she stay inside her garden and stretch over the wall, then feel for the opening in the box and post them, so to speak, upside down? No, she wouldn't be tall enough, would she?

One day she found the answer.

"Take this letter up to the post for me, Janie, will you please?" her mother had

said, and Janie set off, the letter in one
hand, the lead in the other, the collar
around Henry's invisible neck.

She was approaching the postbox
when she saw Mrs Garrow come out of
her front door, also carrying a letter, and
walk across her little bit of lawn to a spot
directly behind the bright red box.

She'll never be able to do it; she's too
short, Janie thought, but then Mrs
Garrow seemed suddenly to rise higher,
and she leaned right over the top of the
wall and posted her letter.

Straightening up, she saw Janie and let
out a burst of quacking laughter.

"Bet you thought I wasn't tall enough

to do that!" she said. "And I wouldn't be if it weren't for these," and Janie could see that the old lady was standing on top of a little pair of wooden steps positioned behind the wall.

"I always enjoy doing that, Janie," Mrs Garrow said. "'Specially as I always feel somehow that the postbox is mine, seeing as it's set in my wall."

"Oh," said Janie. "Is it all right if I post my letter in it?"

"Course it is!" cried Mrs Garrow with another volley of quacks. "Though I'm surprised to see *you* carrying it."

"What d'you mean?" Janie asked.

"Well, I'd have thought that great animal of yours would be carrying it for you in his mouth. Some dogs do, you know. My! He's a size, isn't he? What's his name?"

"Henry," said Janie.

"Well I never!" said Mrs Garrow. "D'you know what, Janie? That was my late husband's name."

"Oh," said Janie. "I'm sorry," she added.

"No need to be sorry, dear," said Mrs Garrow. "He's been dead and gone these twenty years, though never a day passes when I don't think of him. And you know what? There's a lot in common between your Henry and mine."

"How d'you mean?" Janie said.

"Well, my Henry was a great big chap too – he didn't need a step-ladder to post a letter – and another thing, he was quiet, just like your dog. He doesn't bark much, does he?"

"No," Janie said.

"Saw one just like him on the telly, couple of weeks ago," Mrs Garrow said. "Some big dog show it was."

"Cruft's!" said Janie. "We went there!"

"Did you take Henry?"

"No, but there was a dog there just exactly like him and it won the prize for Best of Breed. Another harlequin Great Dane, it was."

"A harlequin Great Dane, eh?" said Mrs Garrow, and she looked down from

her perch at the dangling collar and nodded.

"I see," she said.

"And Daddy says I can have a real one – I mean, another one – but only on one condition."

"And what's that?"

"I have to have five hundred pounds."

"That's a lot of money."

"It's a fortune!"

Mrs Garrow looked down at Janie and her invisible dog, and her wrinkled face creased some more, into a smile.

"Talking of fortunes, Janie," she said, "how would you like me to tell yours?"

"Oh, could you? Oh yes, please," said Janie.

"Come in and have a cup of tea then."

"I'd better ask Mum," said Janie.

"You do that," said Mrs Garrow. "I've got some nice cake."

When Janie returned, permission granted, Mrs Garrow called from her front door, "Come on in."

"What about Henry?" Janie said.

"He'd better stay in the garden," Mrs Garrow said. "My old black cat doesn't like dogs."

"All right," said Janie, and she came in through the gate and dropped the collar and lead on the lawn. "Down, Henry," she said, and "Stay."

"Now," said Mrs Garrow when they had drunk their tea, "let's have a look in your cup."

For a long moment she studied the tea-leaves in the bottom of the cup, very carefully.

Then she said, "Janie, I think you're going to be lucky."

"Why? What can you see?" Janie asked.

"Look," said Mrs Garrow, handing the cup back.

Janie looked in, but all she could see was a scatter of black tea-leaves at the bottom of the white cup.

"I can't see anything," she said.

"You've got to know what you're looking for," said Mrs Garrow. "There's a shape there all right – a great big shape

it is, no doubt about it, and what's more, it's black-and-white."

"A harlequin Great Dane!" cried Janie. "Is that what it is?"

Mrs Garrow smiled her crinkly smile.

"I shouldn't be surprised," she said. "And now you'd best get off home."

Out on the lawn, Janie picked up the end of the lead.

"Heel, Henry!" she said, and "Thank you for the tea, Mrs Garrow. I hope the tea-leaves were right."

"Talking of leaves," said Mrs Garrow, "this lawn's covered in them. I'd better sweep them up. Bye bye, Janie dear."

"Goodbye," Janie said.

For a moment she stood in the lane by the postbox, looking over the low wall. On the lawn old Mrs Garrow was sweeping away with a long broomstick of birch twigs, watched by her black cat.

6. The Money

"I'm bankrupt," said Janie's mother.

"And I soon shall be," said her father. "I don't think it's fair. Whoever heard of a dog playing Monopoly?"

"Specially an invisible dog," his wife said.

Janie sat grinning, a great stack of money in front of her. She patted the unseen head at her side.

"You played well," she said.

It had been Janie's idea that Henry should take part in the game. She threw the dice for him, of course, and moved his symbol round the board, and collected the rents from all his properties as well as her own. As always, she played with the top-hat, her mother with the flat-iron and her father with the car. Henry's symbol had naturally to be the dog.

"OK," said Janie's father as the car landed on Henry's Park Lane hotel. "I've had it too. You win, Janie. You and Henry."

"Cheer up, Daddy," Janie said. "I've got a nice surprise for you," and from a wad of money she peeled off a £500-note and held it out to him.

"What's this for?" he said.

"For my Great Dane puppy.

Remember what you said? 'You come along with five hundred pounds,' you said . . . ''

"Oh, no you don't," her father said. "It's got to be real money if you want a real dog. Five hundred pounds of Monopoly money indeed – you'll be lucky!"

"I think I will be," Janie said.

Later, Janie's mother said, "I wish you hadn't done that silly thing, David."

"What silly thing?"

"Telling Janie she could have a puppy if she had five hundred pounds. You saw the look on her face just now – she genuinely believes she's going to be lucky. It's not fair on the child – there's no way she could find that amount. Either put up the money yourself or shut up about it."

"I just might," Janie's father said.

"Might what? Shut up?"

"No, put up the money. Ever since Janie brought out that lead and collar, I've found myself thinking of dear old Rupert and what a super dog he was and wondering why we never replaced him. And what with Cruft's – well, I must admit I'm getting quite keen on the idea. After all, Sally, we are the right sort of people to have a big dog – we've a sizeable house and garden, we live in the country, and we can afford it."

"You told Janie we couldn't when she first asked you."

"Yes, I know; it's all the fault of that invisible dog of hers. The more she plays that game, the more I find I want to see an actual living, breathing, flesh-and-blood Dane on that lead."

"A harlequin."

"Does that matter? Surely any colour would do."

"Not for Janie it wouldn't. And it may not be easy to find exactly what we want."

"*We?*" said her husband. "You go along with the idea then?"

"We'll see."

"We will," said Janie's father, and he grinned, slyly it seemed to his wife.

"What have you got up your sleeve?" she said.

"Not up my sleeve," said Janie's father. "In my pocket," and he took something out of it.

"What's that?"

"An advertisement. I cut it out of the local paper."

"You don't mean . . . ?"

"Yes. Listen. 'Great Dane puppies for sale. Blacks, blues, one harlequin.'"

"Price?"

"Doesn't say."

"Where?"

"Not all that far away. Extraordinary, isn't it? I had no idea there was a Great Dane breeder anywhere near here. And there's a harlequin in the litter too. What a bit of luck!"

"Janie said she'd be lucky, didn't she?"

"I know. All it needs now is for five hundred pounds to drop out of the sky and land in Janie's lap and I shall begin to believe in witchcraft."

At that instant they heard a loud noise outside.

"What on earth was that?" Janie's father said.

Her mother went to look out of the window.

"Oh, it's only old Mrs Garrow going down the lane," she said. "She has the most peculiar laugh."

"I'll say! I thought it was a duck quacking."

"She's chatting with Janie. And she's flapping her hand up and down. Oh no, I see what she's doing – she's patting Henry."

"That," said Janie's father, "has really made my mind up. If it's got to the stage where Janie's playing her invisible dog game with people like Mrs Garrow, it's high time we got a visible one."

"Will you tell Janie?"

"No, not yet. The harlequin pup may be sold, or it may be a bitch, or it may

just be a poor specimen. We must go and
see the puppies."

"When?"

"As soon as you've taken Janie to
school tomorrow morning."

"But you'll be going to work."

"No. I'm taking the day off. I've fixed
it at the office. Urgent business."

"David! You are a slyboots!"

The postman came just as Janie was
getting ready to go to school next
morning, and by the time their car
reached the top end of the village his van
was parked outside Mrs Garrow's cottage
while he collected the outgoing mail from
the postbox.

Mrs Garrow was chatting to him and
she waved at Janie as they went by.

"Your friend," said Janie's mother.

"She's nice," said Janie, waving back.

"Did you enjoy going to tea with her?"

"Yes, it was interesting."

They drove on, while the postman got into his van and drove away, down towards their house.

7. The Kennels

Back home again, Janie's mother found
her husband still sitting at the breakfast
table, looking very pleased with life. He
waved a letter at her.

"What's up?" his wife said. "You look
as if you've won the pools."

"*I* haven't won anything," Janie's
father said. "Janie has. Do you remember
when she was very small I bought some
Premium Bonds for her? Well, they've
won her some money, quite a nice sum.
Here's the letter telling me so."

"Don't tell me it's five hundred
pounds!"

"No, that would be an unbelievable
coincidence after what I said about
buying a Great Dane puppy."

"How much then?"

"Two hundred."

"It won't be enough then," Janie's mother said.

"Enough for what?"

"Why, to buy one of those puppies. For Janie to buy one, I mean, with her own money."

They looked at one another.

"We might have to add a bit to it," Janie's father said.

74

They looked at one another again, and they smiled.

"Ring up the kennels," Janie's mother said, "and see if they'll keep the harlequin until we get there."

She listened anxiously to her husband's share of the conversation.

"Good morning. I'm inquiring about the pups you advertised. Are they sold?"

. . .

"I see. But you still have the harlequin?"

. . .

"Dog or bitch?"

. . .

"Oh, good. That's the one we're interested in. Can you keep him for us?"

. . .

"Yes, I understand. We must take a chance on that. We'll be with you just as soon as we can. By the way, how much are you asking for him?"

The answer to this last question seemed to take some time, but at last Janie's father put the phone down.

"The harlequin is a dog puppy," he said, "and he's not sold. The woman said she couldn't guarantee to keep him for us. She's sold a couple of the others but hasn't had anyone after the harlequin yet."

76

"How much?" Janie's mother said.
"She seemed to take a lot of time
answering when you asked her that."

"That's because she was giving me a
long spiel about how well bred this litter
is, and what the mother had won, and
the fact that the father is Champion
Thingummy Nobleman of Wotsitsname –
you know, the dog that won at Cruft's."

"So, how much?"

"Five hundred pounds."

"I'm awfully sorry," the breeder said when they arrived. "No sooner had you rung off than someone turned up, wanting the harlequin puppy. He's just this moment driven off; you probably passed him on your way here."

Janie's parents looked at one another once more, and they sighed a joint sigh.

"There are still two blacks and a blue left," said the breeder.

"No," Janie's mother said, "thanks all the same. It has to be a harlequin or nothing."

"Leave me your address and phone number then," said the breeder. "I might hear of something."

"At least Janie doesn't know anything

about it," said one to the other as they drove home again, "so she won't be disappointed."

"And she's got a nice surprise waiting for her when she gets back from school this afternoon."

"I didn't even know I had a Premium Bond," Janie said when they showed her the letter and the cheque. "You never told me."

"We don't tell you everything," her father said.

"Two hundred pounds!" Janie said. "Nearly enough to buy half a harlequin Great Dane puppy!"

"Has it really *got* to be a harlequin?" her mother said.

"Yes. She said so."

"Who said so?"

"Mrs Garrow."

"What on earth has Mrs Garrow got to do with it?"

"She saw it."

"I don't know *what* you're talking about," her father said.

After tea Janie took the invisible dog for a walk up the lane. As she passed Mrs Garrow's cottage, the old lady looked over the garden wall and said, "Hullo, Janie. Better luck next time."

I don't know what you're talking about, Janie thought.

"Ask your mum and dad," Mrs Garrow said, just as though she'd read Janie's mind.

"Ask them what?"

"Where they went this morning."

"Where did you go this morning?" Janie asked when she got home again.

"How d'you know we went
anywhere?" her father said.

"I just do."

There was a pause.

"Tell her," her mother said.

At that moment the phone rang. It was
the Great Dane breeder.

"I've just this minute had a thought," she said. "Since you just missed that puppy this morning and are set on having a harlequin, I've had an idea, if you're interested. I have a nine-month-old harlequin dog that might do you. He's a good typical specimen, with a

lovely nature, but he has a fault that spoils him for the show-ring."

"What sort of fault?" Janie's mother said.

"He's got a kink in his tail – a little sort of twist near the end of it. He was born like that, but I've kept him on because he's such a lovable character. Would you like to see him?"

They arrived once more at the kennels, this time with Janie. The breeder looked at her as she stood, lead in hand, collar dangling. "That's a biggish collar," she said. "Have you had a Dane before?"

"We had one called Rupert," Janie said, "when I was very small, but he was fawn, not a harlequin like this one."

"Which one?" said the breeder.

"Janie has an invisible dog," her father said. "He goes everywhere with her. He's never any trouble."

"Sit, Henry!" Janie said.

"Did you say Henry?" said the breeder. "How extraordinary! Hang on half a tick, I'll fetch the dog."

Of course they all fell in love with him at first sight. Already he seemed enormous, with feet like soup-plates. He did not squirm or wriggle as a puppy would have done, but stood steady in black-and-white dignity as befitted someone who was almost grown-up.

"His nose is partly black and partly pink!" Janie's father said as the young dog sniffed at them.

"That's all right," the breeder said. "A harlequin's allowed a butterfly nose."

"And he's got one brown eye and one blue!" said Janie's mother, as he smiled at them.

"A wall eye. That's all right too. He's a good typical specimen, with a lovely nature, but, like I said, he has a kink in his tail – that little sort of twist near the end of it."

As if he understood, the dog slowly wagged his tail.

"I like that," Janie said. "I want to buy him, please."

"*You* want to?" the breeder said, smiling. "Have you got enough money of your own, d'you think?"

"I've got two hundred pounds," Janie said.

"I won't charge you that much," the breeder said. "As I told you, he's no good for show, with that fault. But I don't think I can give him to you – he's cost me a lot to rear. On the other hand, I feel sure that you'll give him a really good home. So shall we say a hundred pounds?"

Janie put out a hand.

"It's a deal," she said. "What's he called?"

"You aren't going to believe it," the breeder said. "In fact I must confess that there's something very strange about all this. But he's called Henry."

Janie nodded. It was as though she had expected this news.

Carefully she unbuckled the collar from the invisible dog and fastened it again around the neck of his successor. "Good boy, Henry," she said.

8. The Twist

About a week later Janie came out of the
front gate and turned up the lane, the
lead in her right hand, her dog walking
steadily at heel with his long strides, his
great head not far below her shoulder.
From the buckle of his collar hung a new
round metal disc that said, above the
telephone number, HENRY.

They walked up the village until they came to Mrs Garrow's wall, with the red postbox set into it, and Janie opened the garden gate and went in. Inside the porch of the cottage were Mrs Garrow's wellies and, leaning in the corner, the long broomstick that she used for sweeping up leaves. Her cat sat on the mat.

"My old black cat doesn't like dogs," Mrs Garrow had said, but to Janie's surprise it stood up and began to rub itself against one of Henry's long legs, purring loudly. Henry looked embarrassed.

Janie knocked on the front door, and after a moment old Mrs Garrow opened it, smiling her crinkly smile.

"Hullo," Janie said. "This is Henry."

"I know that, dear," said Mrs Garrow. "You showed him to me before, lots

of times, don't you remember?"

She patted the dog.

"Who's a good boy then?" she said. "He's looking ever so well, Janie. You must be proud of him."

"I am," Janie said. "D'you see, he's got a butterfly nose and a wall eye?

There's only one thing meant to be wrong with him though I don't think it matters a bit, and that's the twist in his tail."

"It was all in the tea-leaves," Mrs Garrow said.

"I don't understand," Janie said. "How can you know these things?"

Mrs Garrow let out her usual volley of quacks.

"Aha, Janie my dear!" she said. "That's the twist in the tale."

The Swoose

Dick King-Smith

"Are you feather-brained?" said the vole. "No, I'm Fitzherbert."

Fitzherbert is confused. With his oversized feet and snaky neck, he is shunned by the other goslings. Then his mother reveals that he is a rare breed of bird indeed – the offspring of her romantic liaison with a dashing white swan. With stars in his eyes, Fitzherbert sets off in search of his father and discovers fame beyond the farmyard in the household of the Queen of England herself!

'Other writers who put words into animals' mouths are outclassed'
– *The Times Educational Supplement*

'Judy Brown's enchanting black and white illustrations capture the spirit of both swoose and sovereign'
– *Independent on Sunday*

A Narrow

Squeak

and Other Animal Stories

Dick King-Smith

Be they soft and furry, sharp and prickly or smooth and scaly, all the animals in this collection are quite irresistible!

A mouse is dicing with death in the larder, while another is carried off in the jaws of a fox. Then there's a bullied brontosaurus, a wimpish woodlouse, a rebellious hedgehog and a dog with an identity crisis.

'Other writers who put words into animals' mouths are outclassed' – *The Times Educational Supplement*

Also in Young Puffin

GEORGE SPEAKS

Dick King-Smith

Laura's baby brother George was four weeks old when it happened.

George looks like an ordinary baby, with his round red face and squashy nose. But Laura soon discovers that he's absolutely *extraordinary*, and everyone's life is turned upside down from the day George speaks!

Also in Young Puffin

The Ghost *at* Codlin Castle
and Other Stories

Dick King-Smith

Have you ever wondered what it's like to carry your head under your arm? Or tried to guess what garden gnomes get up to after dark?

In this marvellously varied collection of stories, Dick King-Smith introduces some fascinating characters: a baby yeti, a bald hobgoblin and an extraordinary sausage-shaped alien among them.

Funny, mysterious, sinister, these gripping tales make ideal bedtime reading. With remarkable illustrations by Amanda Harvey, this is a book to stir the imagination.

Also in Young Puffin

THE Hodgeheg

Dick King-Smith

**Max is a hedgehog who becomes a
hodgeheg, who becomes a hero!**

The hedgehog family of Number 5A are a
happy bunch, but they dream of reaching
the Park. Unfortunately, a very busy
road lies between them and their goal and
no one has found a way to cross it in
safety. No one, that is, until the
determined young Max decides to solve
the problem once and for all...

READ MORE IN PUFFIN

For children of all ages, Puffin represents quality and variety – the very best in publishing today around the world.

For complete information about books available from Puffin – and Penguin – and how to order them, contact us at the appropriate address below. Please note that for copyright reasons the selection of books varies from country to country.

On the world wide web: www.penguin.co.uk

In the United Kingdom: Please write to *Dept. EP, Penguin Books Ltd, Bath Road, Harmondsworth, West Drayton, Middlesex UB7 ODA*

In the United States: Please write to *Consumer Sales, Penguin USA, P.O. Box 999, Dept. 17109, Bergenfield, New Jersey 07621-0120*. VISA and MasterCard holders call 1-800-253-6476 to order Penguin titles

In Canada: Please write to *Penguin Books Canada Ltd, 10 Alcorn Avenue, Suite 300, Toronto, Ontario M4V 3B2*

In Australia: Please write to *Penguin Books Australia Ltd, P.O. Box 257, Ringwood, Victoria 3134*

In New Zealand: Please write to *Penguin Books (NZ) Ltd, Private Bag 102902, North Shore Mail Centre, Auckland 10*

In India: Please write to *Penguin Books India Pvt Ltd, 706 Eros Apartments, 56 Nehru Place, New Delhi 110 019*

In the Netherlands: Please write to *Penguin Books Netherlands bv, Postbus 3507, NL-1001 AH Amsterdam*

In Germany: Please write to *Penguin Books Deutschland GmbH, Metzlerstrasse 26, 60594 Frankfurt am Main*

In Spain: Please write to *Penguin Books S. A., Bravo Murillo 19, 1° B, 28015 Madrid*

In Italy: Please write to *Penguin Italia s.r.l., Via Felice Casati 20, I–20124 Milano*

In France: Please write to *Penguin France S. A., 17 rue Lejeune, F–31000 Toulouse*

In Japan: Please write to *Penguin Books Japan, Ishikiribashi Building, 2–5–4, Suido, Bunkyo-ku, Tokyo 112*

In South Africa: Please write to *Longman Penguin Southern Africa (Pty) Ltd, Private Bag X08, Bertsham 2013*